His Cherished Soul

Vol. 1, "Soul Searching"

Story and art: E J Lutze

His Cherished Soul: Soul Searching is ©2024 EJ Lutze. All rights reserved.

Ghosts

The final remnants of living creatures

Desperately clinging to their connections to the living world

connections like strings

Cut the strings...

...no more ghost

But then...

But if a soul is pulled away

Like a loose thread...

Discarded from its vessel

"Wobble"
"Wobble"

SNAP!

Before it is meant to...

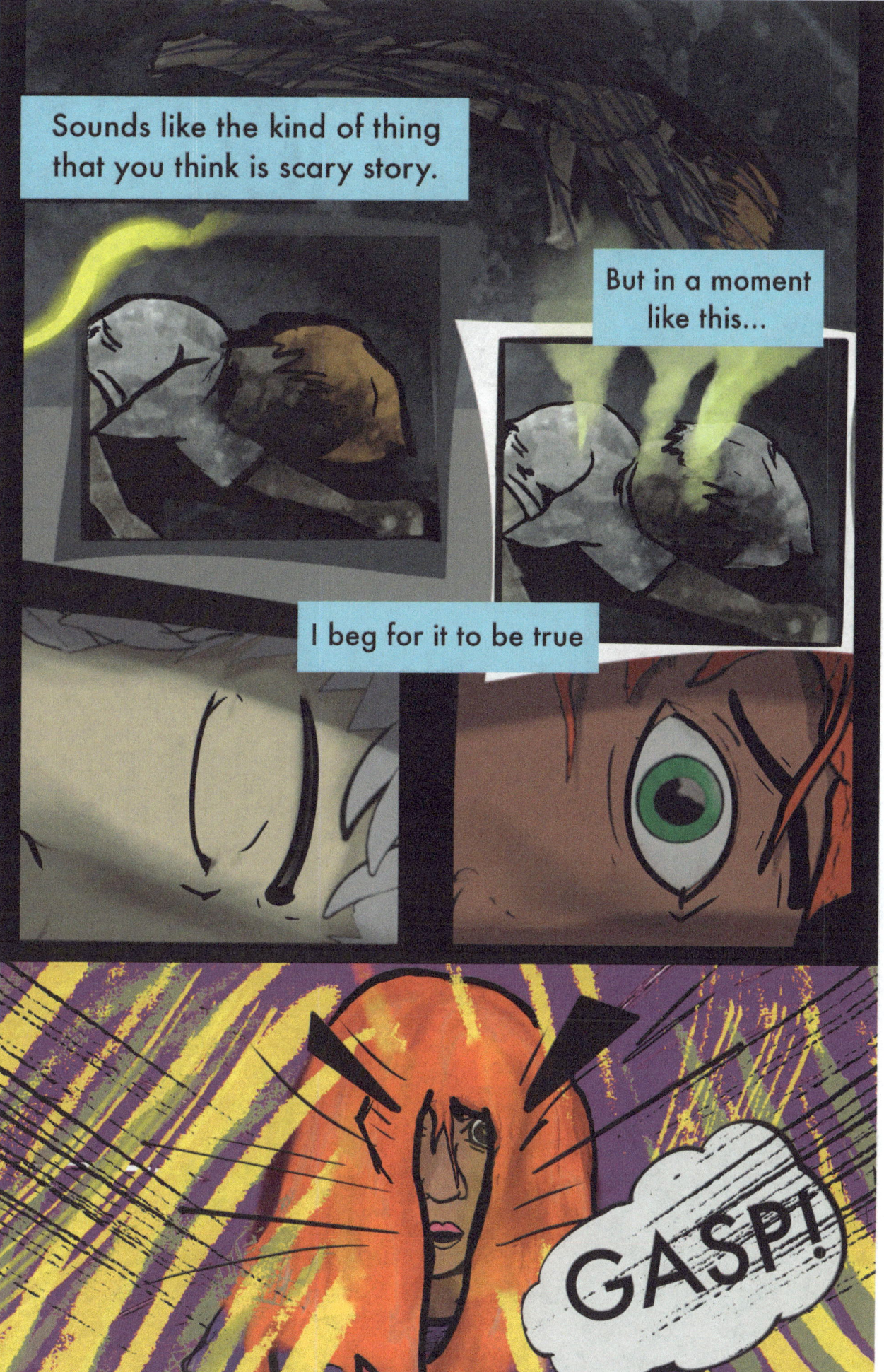

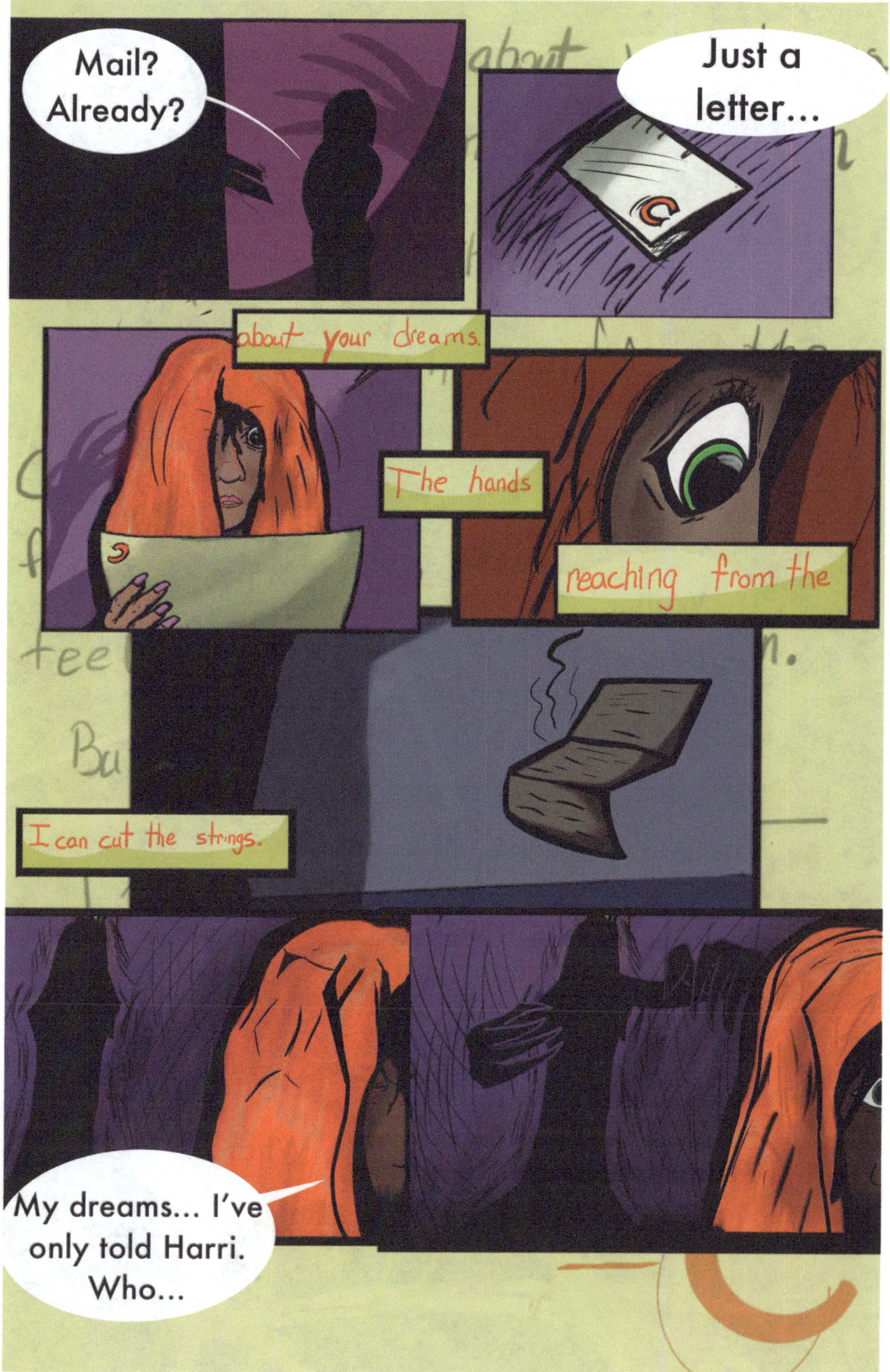

Ggyyaaahhh!

Aunt Terri!

The charm!

Got it!

Woah!

Snap

I alway get hit...

SLAM

Ough!

But this hurts.

A lot.

Did I get it?

I'll see you burn for thiiiiisss....

Sounds like it.

Hello?

Lane!
Lane, your aunt...

She- she...

Oh, Lane...

She died...

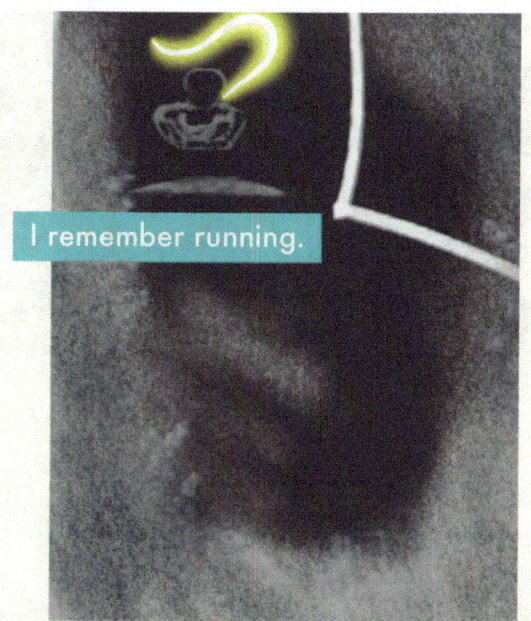

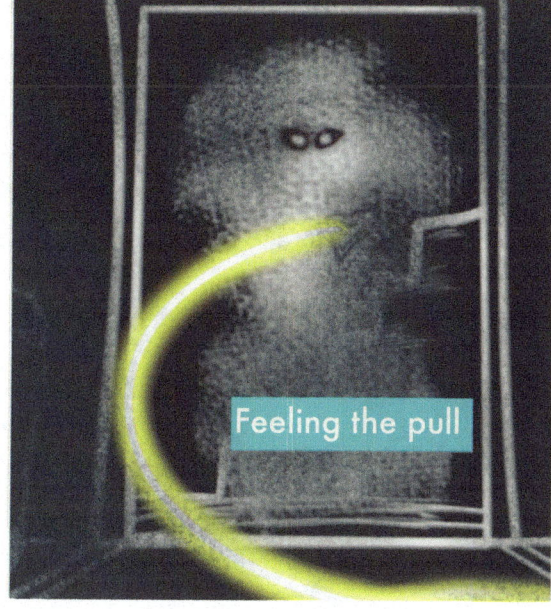

It was terrifying. She was thrashing so much.

Throwing herself into the air...

Her hands were out like she was fighting someone.

She was screaming in pain.

Then she fell back...

SNAP

...And it all stopped...

"But not right now, Harri dear"

Swish

"Harri, I'll meet you in a minute"

"I need to say something to Lane"

"Okay... I... need to get some air anyway..."

It was the same necklace. The same kind anyway.

"You seem so upset. More than usual. This should be normal by now."

What? Is she talking about dad?

I felt like I was being paranoid. After that morning, nothing made sense.

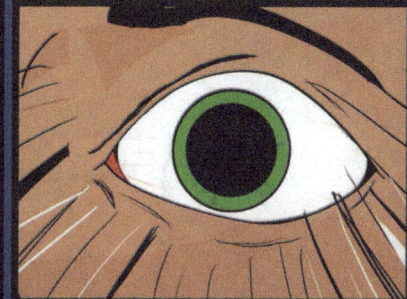

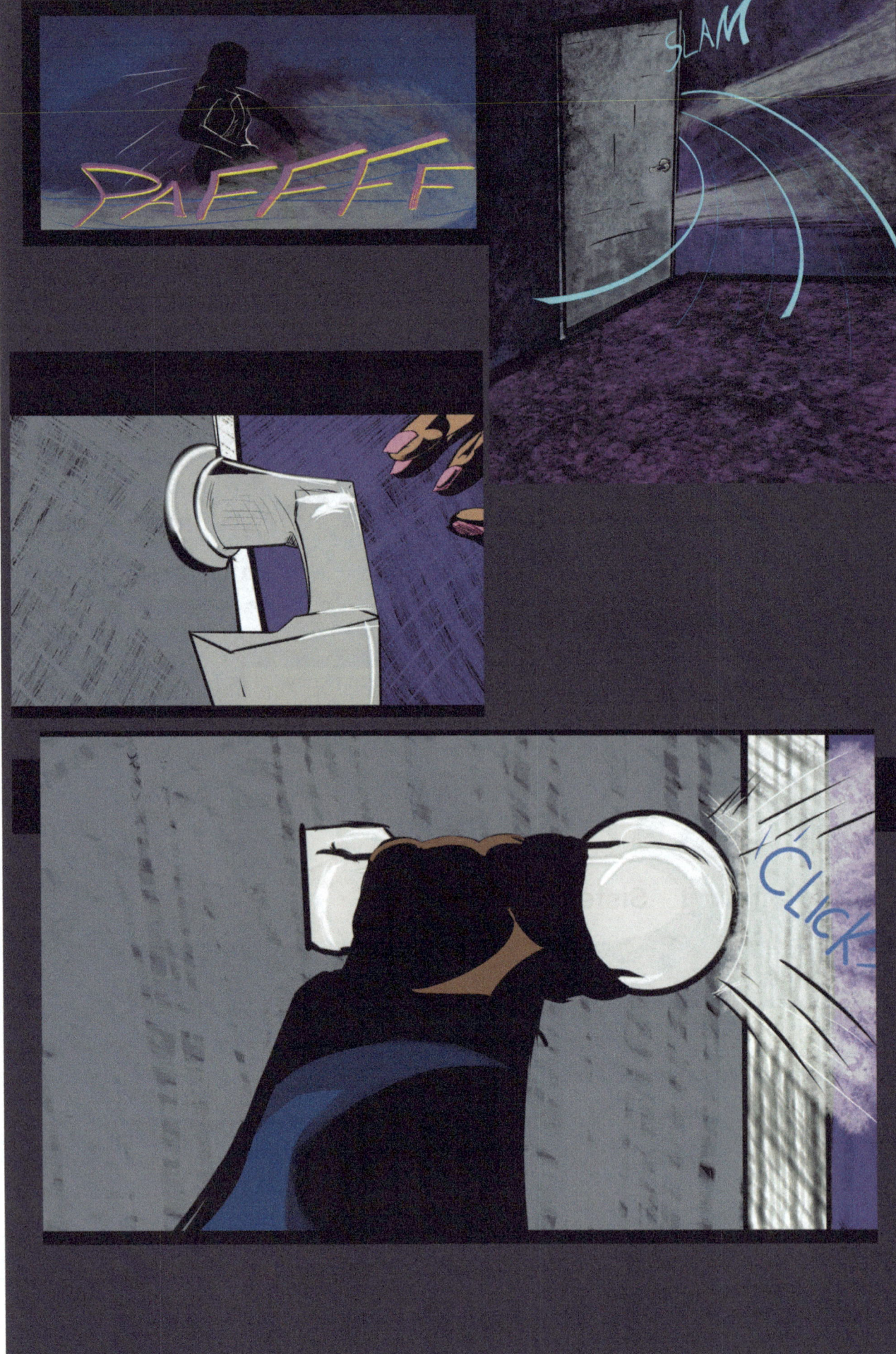

They were right there...

Then they were gone.

Harri...

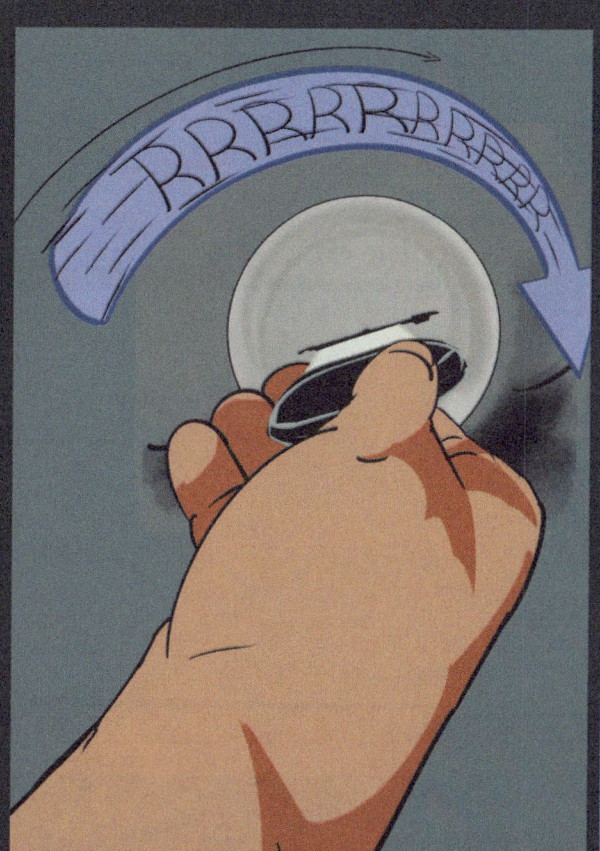

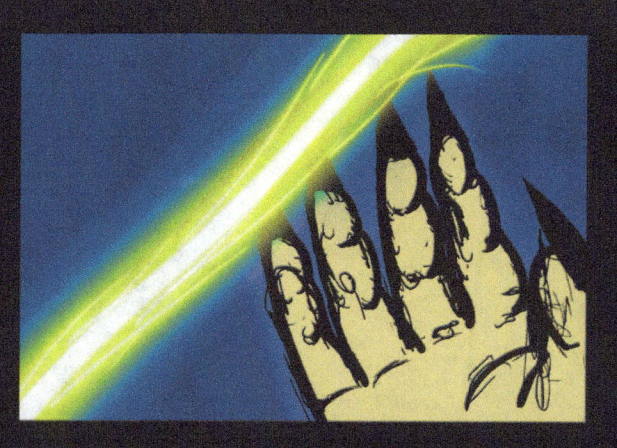

Made in the USA
Monee, IL
06 February 2025

11054132R00066